Nate the Great
and the
Mushy Valentine

Nate the Great

and the

Mushy Valentine

by Marjorie Weinman Sharmat
illustrated by Marc Simont

A YEARLING BOOK

Text copyright © 1994 by Marjorie Weinman Sharmat
Cover art and interior illustrations copyright © 1994 by Marc Simont
Extra Fun Activities text copyright © 2004 by Emily Costello
Extra Fun Activities illustrations copyright © 2004 by Jody Wheeler

Yearling and the jumping horse design are registered trademarks of Penguin Random House LLC.

Visit us on the Web! randomhousekids.com

Educators and librarians, for a variety of teaching tools, visit us at RHTeachersLibrarians.com

Library of Congress Cataloging-in-Publication Data is available upon request.
ISBN 978-0-385-31166-3 (trade) — ISBN 978-0-440-41013-3 (pbk.)
— ISBN 978-0-385-37298-5 (ebook)

Printed in the United States of America
40   39

First Yearling Edition 1995

For my two Nates:

For you, my grandson,
Nathan Sharmat,
born December 12, 1992

And in memory of your
great-grandfather,
Nathan Weinman,
born one hundred years earlier
on July 12, 1892

Always remember, Nate is great!

My name is Nate the Great.
I am a detective.
I have a dog, Sludge.
He is a detective too.
He helps me with my cases.
But one day I had to help
Sludge with his case.

It was Valentine's Day.
Sludge was napping
in his doghouse.
I tiptoed up to it.
I saw a big red paper heart
taped to the outside of the house.
Something was printed on the heart.
I LOVE YOU SLUDGE
MORE THAN FUDGE.
Someone had given Sludge
a valentine!
I was glad that no one had given me
a valentine.
I, Nate the Great, do not like
mushy words.
Or slushy words.
I, Nate the Great, do not want to be
anyone's valentine.

Sludge came out of his doghouse.

I showed him his valentine.

It was signed with initials.

ABH.

"Who is ABH?" I asked Sludge.

Sludge sniffed the valentine.

And sniffed it.

He did not know who it was from, either.

He looked at me.

"You want me to help you
find out who sent you
this valentine?" I asked.
"This is not my kind of case."
But Sludge is my kind of dog.
I wrote a note to my mother.

Dear Mother,
I am on a Valentine case.
Somebody loves Sludge
more than fudge.
When I find out who
I will be back.
Love,
Nate the Great

Sludge and I looked for
footprints around his doghouse.
Sludge carried his valentine
in his mouth
while he looked.
He liked it.
We did not see any footprints.
I was thinking,
What clues do I have?

The printing on the valentine
was made with stencils.
Anybody could have done it.
And anybody could have
stuck the valentine
on the doghouse.
Who do Sludge and I know?
We know Rosamond, Oliver, Claude,
Annie, Annie's little brother Harry,
Esmeralda, Pip, and Finley.
None of them have the initials ABH.
I saw Annie and her dog, Fang,
coming toward us.
Fang will never be anybody's
valentine.
"I have a case for you," Annie said.
"I can't find a valentine that I made.
Please look for it."

"I already have a valentine case,"
I said. "Somebody gave Sludge
a valentine, but we don't know who.
I, Nate the Great,
take only one case at a time."
"I must find my valentine,"
Annie said. *"Please."*
I wrote another note to my mother.

Dear Mother
Two Valentine cases.
I will be back.
Love,
Nate the Great

"Tell me about your missing
valentine," I said to Annie.
"This morning Rosamond and I each
made a valentine at my house,"
Annie said. "Rosamond called them
valentwins."
"Valentwins?"
"Yes, because her valentine and my
valentine looked exactly alike.
We each cut out a big red paper heart.
We each printed I LOVE YOU
on our hearts."
"Then what happened?" I asked.
"Rosamond went home with
her valentine,"
Annie said. "I began to sign my name
on mine. I was going to give it
to my little brother Harry.

But Fang came into my room.
He looked hungry."
I, Nate the Great,
knew that look very well.
"Fang and I went to the kitchen,"
Annie said. "I gave him some kibbles.
When I got back to my room,
my valentine was gone."

"Did Rosamond tell you who she was making her valentine for?" I asked.

"No," Annie said. "What does that have to do with my case?"

"Nothing," I said. "But I am on two cases at the same time. Remember?" I pointed to Sludge. "Please look at the valentine Sludge is carrying. Does that look like the ones that you and Rosamond made?"

"Yes," Annie said. "Except that there's more printed on this one. And this one also has initials. Rosamond's valentine and my valentine just said I LOVE YOU."

"But then you started to sign yours," I said.

"Yes, but I didn't get very far,"
Annie said.

"*You* may not have gotten very far,"
I said, "but Rosamond could have
printed much more on *her* valentine
when she got home. I, Nate the Great,

say that Rosamond made her
valentine for Sludge."
"Why would she do that?"
Annie asked.
"Only Rosamond knows," I said.
"Last year she made a valentine
for the man in the moon."
"So you have solved your case,"
Annie said.
"Not quite," I said.
"Sludge's valentine
was signed with the initials ABH.

Those are not Rosamond's initials.
Why would she print them on her
valentine? Before I solve a case, all the
pieces have to fit."

"Do you have any clues in *my* case?"
Annie asked.

"I don't know. Show me where your
valentine was the last time you saw it."
We all walked to Annie's house.

We went to her room.
She pointed to her desk.
"The valentine was right here,"
she said.
I looked at Annie's desk.
There were pencils
and stencils and paste
and red paper on it.
No valentine.
Sludge was sniffing the desk.
"There are no clues
on this desk,"
I said to him.

But Sludge kept sniffing.
I peered over and under,
in back of, in front of,
and inside of things.
I could not find Annie's valentine.

"Your valentine is not in this room,"
I said. "Tell me, was anybody
in your house besides you and Fang
when your valentine disappeared?"
"Yes," Annie said. "Harry was
in his room."
"Hmm. He could have gone to your
room while you were in the kitchen."
"I suppose," Annie said. "But he
wouldn't have taken the valentine.
He knew I was going to give it to him
right after I finished signing
my name to it."
"Perhaps he was in a hurry to
have it," I said.
"No," Annie said. "Harry doesn't like
valentines."

"Then why did you make one for him?"
I asked.

Annie smiled. "I like to give
valentines."

"So you like to give but Harry doesn't
like to get," I said. "That could be
important. Then again, it might not
be important. I must talk to Harry.
Where is he?"

Annie shrugged. "He disappeared
when the valentine disappeared."
"Aha!" I said. "That could be
a big clue. Where does Harry
like to go?"
"He likes to go to Rosamond's house
to play with her Hexes," Annie said.
"Her Hexes?"
"You know, Rosamond's cats.
She has a Super Hex, a Big Hex,
a Plain Hex, and a Little Hex."
"Yes," I said. "Rosamond has a Hex
for all occasions."

Suddenly I, Nate the Great, thought
of something.
"I have just solved the case," I said.
"Oh, great," Annie said. "Where is
my valentine?"
"No, not your case. Sludge's case.
I have not been thinking strange enough.
If I had, I would have known that
the pieces fit. I must speak to
Rosamond."
"And look for Harry," Annie said.
I, Nate the Great, do not like
to go to Rosamond's house.
But now I had two reasons to go there.
Annie, Sludge, Fang, and I rushed
to Rosamond's house.

Rosamond was sitting on her floor,
making a strange, squishy brown
valentine. Her four cats were crawling
all over her.

"I am on two cases," I said. "I need
Harry for one and you for the other."

"Harry was here playing with my

cats," Rosamond said. "But he left.
I don't know where he went.
But I'm here. Why do you need me?"
I took Sludge's valentine
from his mouth.

I handed it to Rosamond.

"I, Nate the Great, say that you
made this valentine for Sludge
and signed it ABH. Those are
the initials for *A Big Hex*.
This valentine was from Big Hex
to Sludge, right?"

"Wrong," Rosamond said. "This
valentine looks like the one I made,
except for the Sludge part and the
initials."

"You didn't add words or initials
to yours?" I asked.

"I added words," Rosamond said.
"But these are not the words.
Besides, I would never
do a strange thing

like make a valentine
for a cat to give to a dog."
Rosamond would do even stranger
things, but I did not want to
go into that.
"I made my valentine for a
person," Rosamond said, "but
it's a secret who. Right now
I am making a valentine out of liver
for my cats. They haven't
been eating their liver lately.

It's too good to throw away,
so I am changing it into
something different.
Want to watch my cats
eat their valentine?"
It was time to leave.
I said to Annie, "Go to your house
and wait there,
in case Harry comes back."
Sludge and I went home.
"I have to eat pancakes,"
I said to Sludge. "I have to think.
I have to think twice as hard
as I would if I had only
one case to solve."
I made some pancakes.
I gave Sludge a bone.
I thought about Sludge's case.

Sludge is a great dog.

Everybody loves him.

Anybody could have given him

the valentine.

That was no help to me.

I thought about Annie's case.
The only person who
could have taken the valentine
meant for Harry
was Harry.
But Annie said that Harry
doesn't like valentines.
I made more pancakes.
What had I learned at
Rosamond's house?
I learned what she did with liver
that her cats didn't want.

If that was a clue, it was a strange one.
What had I learned at Annie's house?
Sludge had kept sniffing
at Annie's desk.
Where her valentine had been.
Was that a clue?
Perhaps.
But what case was it a clue for?
Sludge's case?

Or Annie's case?

Or *both*?

Did it matter?

Perhaps I could use a clue from
one case to help solve another case!
I picked up Sludge's valentine
where he had dropped it
while he chewed his bone.
There *had* to be a reason
why Sludge's valentine looked
like Annie's and Rosamond's.
But Rosamond said she had made hers
for a secret person.
And Annie said she had made hers
for her brother Harry.
I stared at the initials ABH.
I now knew they didn't mean
A Big Hex.

But they had to be *somebody's* initials.
Who would sign ABH?
Suddenly I, Nate the Great, had a lot
of pieces that fit.
"We must go back to Annie's house,"
I said.
Sludge dropped his bone and
picked up his valentine.
We went to Annie's house.

Sludge sniffed Annie's desk again.
"I have solved your case,"
I said to Annie. "See how
Sludge is sniffing your desk?
That's because *his* valentine
was once on your desk.
His valentine was *your*
valentine."

"What?" Annie said.
"How much of your name did you
print on your valentine before
you had to stop?" I asked.
"Just A," Annie said. "I was going
to finish with NNIE."

"I, Nate the Great, say that your
brother Harry saw the valentine
you made for him. He didn't want
it. So he added the words
SLUDGE MORE THAN FUDGE.
Then he added B and H to the A
you had signed. ABH stands for
Annie's Brother Harry. Then he
took the valentine to Sludge's
doghouse and stuck it there."

"But why didn't he just throw away
the valentine instead of doing all
of that?" Annie asked.
"For the same reason Rosamond
could not throw away the liver,"
I said. "Remember when she told us
it was too good to throw away,
so she changed it into something
different? Harry did not want to
throw away something good, either:

the valentine you made for him.
So he changed it into something
different . . . a valentine for Sludge."
"But why Sludge?" Annie asked.
"Look how much Sludge likes it,"
I said. "Harry had a very good idea."
"I will never make another valentine
for Harry," Annie said.
"Harry will be glad to hear that,"
I said. I turned to go.
I had solved Annie's case.
I had solved Sludge's case.
They were the same case.
Sludge and I walked home.
I saw something
stuck to my front door.

It was a big red paper heart.

I had gotten a valentine after all!

I knew who it was from.

I knew what I did not want
to know.

I was Rosamond's secret person.

I walked up to the door.

I, Nate the Great,
was about to read that
Rosamond loves me.

I was not ready for that.

I would never be ready for that.

But I had to face it.

I read I LOVE YOU NATE
BECAUSE YOU'RE GREAT.

I had to take this valentine
off my door!

But if I touched it,
it would be mine.
Perhaps the valentine would fall off
by itself.
Or blow away.
Rot.
Die.

I, Nate the Great, could wait.
I stepped backward.
I knew another house
where I could wait.
Sludge was very glad to have me.

~ Extra ~
Fun Activities!

What's Inside

NATE'S NOTES: Valentine's Day

People send more than a billion Valentine's Day cards each year. Most of those people are girls and women.

People also send flowers on Valentine's Day. Loads of flowers—including about 110 million roses.

Long ago, an emperor lived in Rome. He thought more men would be soldiers if they couldn't have families. So he banned marriage.

A man called Valentine helped people get married anyway.

The emperor got mad. He threw Valentine in jail.

Valentine fell in love with his guard's daughter. He wrote her mushy letters from jail.

Valentine's Day is probably named after this man.

Rosamond is weird. But she's not alone. Lots of people give their pets valentines.

The first Valentine's Day card was sent in the year 1415.

Americans spend more than a billion dollars on candy each Valentine's Day.

The bestselling Valentine candy? "Sweethearts"—those tiny hearts with words. The NECCO company has made them since 1866. NECCO makes about 8 billion Sweethearts each year.

The human mouth is just warm enough to melt chocolate.

Hershey's makes more than 80 million "Kisses" every day.

Americans buy 36 million heart-shaped boxes of chocolate every Valentine's Day.

Eating chocolate can make you feel as if you're falling in love. Yuck!

Check Your Valentine Smarts

Are you as smart as Nate? Prove it by answering these Valentine questions. It's okay to look for the answers in a book. Or check the Web.

1. When is Valentine's Day celebrated?
   a. the first Tuesday in February
   b. February 14
   c. February 15

2. Who gets the most Valentines?
   a. math teachers
   b. moms and dads
   c. dogs named Fang
   d. space aliens

3. Which of the following is not a popular Valentine's gift?
   a. liver
   b. chocolate
   c. flowers

4. Which flower is popular on Valentine's Day?
   a. red rose
   b. purple lily
   c. cactus flower

5. What does the letter X mean at the bottom
   of a valentine?
   a. buried treasure
   b. a kiss
   c. the mark of Zorro

6. Who was Valentine?
   a. an outfielder for the Yankees
   b. a man who helped Romans get married
   c. a singer

7. When do people buy the most candy?
   a. Valentine's Day
   b. Halloween
   c. Thanksgiving

8. You shouldn't give chocolate to a dog. Why?
   a. It hurts the dog's kidneys and heart.
   b. The cats will get jealous.
   c. Dogs prefer jelly beans.

9. In what country do people eat the most chocolate?
   a. The United States
   b. Switzerland
   c. Australia

10. Where is the biggest chocolate factory in the world?
   a. London
   b. Mexico City
   c. Hershey, Pennsylvania

Answers: 1. b; 2. b; 3. a; 4. a; 5. b; 6. b; 7. b; 8. a; 9. b; 10. c.

Valentine Riddles

What did the elephant
say to his valentine?
I love you a ton.

What did the pickle say
to her valentine?
You mean a great dill to me.

What did the octopus say
to his valentine?
*I want to hold your hand,
hand, hand, hand, hand,
hand, hand, hand.*

What did the farmer
give his valentine?
Hogs and kisses.

How to Make Love Bugs

Valentines aren't all hearts and flowers. These look like bugs!

GET TOGETHER:

- plastic spoons
- newspaper
- ready-to-use plaster of Paris*
- a butter knife
- small magnets*
- Q-tips or paintbrushes
- paint
- glue
- wiggle eyes*

* You can buy these things in a crafts store.

HOW TO MAKE YOUR LOVE BUG VALENTINES:

1. Lay the spoons out on the newspaper.
2. Fill each spoon with plaster of Paris. Level with the butter knife.
3. Wait about 2 minutes. Press a small magnet into each spoonful of plaster of Paris.
4. Let dry completely.
5. Push on the edges of the spoons to pop out the plaster "bugs." Smooth the edges with the butter knife.
6. Using Q-tips or paintbrushes, paint the bugs red and black like real ladybugs. Or use other colors to invent new bugs.
7. Let the paint dry.
8. Glue on wiggle eyes.

Annie's Chocolate Dip Recipe

Making dip helps Annie get into the Valentine's Day spirit. (Nate prefers pancakes.)

GET TOGETHER:

- a cookie sheet
- waxed paper
- a small (6-ounce) package of chocolate chips
- a glass bowl
- strawberries, apple slices, banana slices, grapes
- a rubber spatula

HOW TO MAKE YOUR DIP:

1. Cover the cookie sheet with waxed paper.
2. Pour the chocolate chips into the glass bowl.
3. Microwave on high for 30 seconds.

4. Using oven mitts, remove the bowl from the microwave. Stir the chips with the rubber spatula.

5. Microwave on high for another 30 seconds. Remove. Stir.

6. Repeat until the chocolate just BEGINS to melt. Be careful not to let it get too hot.

7. Stir until the lumps disappear. If you need to, microwave for a few more seconds. Let the chocolate cool for a minute.

8. Dip the fruit into the cooled melted chocolate. Place on the waxed paper.

9. Set aside for about 2 hours, until the chocolate gets hard.

10. Eat!

More Valentine Riddles

What did the stamp say to the envelope?
Stick with me and we'll go places.

What travels around the world but stays in one corner?
A stamp.

What does an envelope say when you lick it?
It shuts up.

Knock
knock.
Who's there?
Olive.
Olive who?
Olive you!

Jell-O Hearts Recipe

*Jell-O hearts are a nice snack
to have while making valentines.*

GET TOGETHER:

- 2 large boxes of strawberry or cherry Jell-O
- 2½ cups of boiling water
- unflavored cooking spray
- a large rectangular pan
- a spatula
- a heart-shaped cookie cutter

HOW TO MAKE YOUR JELL-O HEARTS:

1. Pour the Jell-O powder into a bowl.
2. Add the boiling water.
3. Stir until the Jell-O dissolves completely.
4. Spray the pan lightly with the cooking spray.
5. Pour the Jell-O into the pan.
6. Chill the pan in the refrigerator for at least 3 hours.
7. Cut out Jell-O hearts with the cookie cutter.
8. Lift the hearts from the pan with the spatula. Place on a pretty plate and serve to your valentine.

HOW TO MAKE YOUR GRASS HEART:

1. Use the pen and the cookie cutter to trace a heart shape onto the sponge. Cut out the shape.
2. Rinse the sponge. Let dry.
3. Put the sponge inside the cookie cutter. Place on a plastic plate.
4. Sprinkle grass seed on the sponge. Spray the seed lightly with water. Cover with plastic wrap.
5. When shoots appear, remove the plastic wrap.
6. Remind your valentine to spray with water every day. Your valentine can also "mow" his or her heart with scissors.

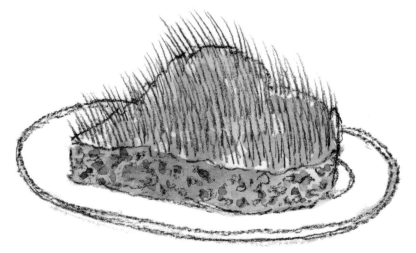

Mailing a Valentine

*Almost a billion valentines are mailed each year!
How do all those cards get where they're going?
Read on to find out.*

PARTS OF AN ENVELOPE

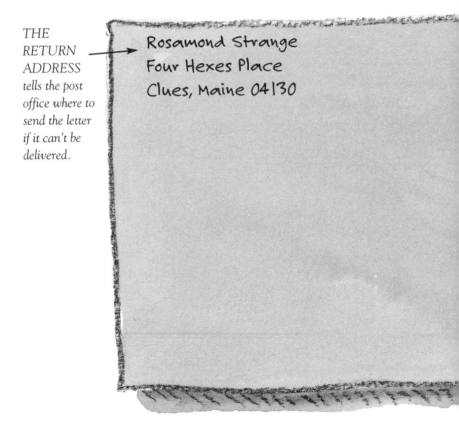

THE
RETURN
ADDRESS
*tells the post
office where to
send the letter
if it can't be
delivered.*

Rosamond Strange
Four Hexes Place
Clues, Maine 04130

THE STAMP *pays to have the letter delivered. The United States Postal Service prints special heart stamps for Valentine's Day.*

Nate the Great
24 Sleuth Street
Clues, Maine 04130

THE ADDRESS: *The first line of the address is the name of the person who will get the card. The second line should include the person's house number and street. Next line: city, state, and zip code.*

THE ZIP CODE *is a code with five numbers. It helps postal workers sort the mail.*

How Valentines Travel

STEP ONE: You mail a valentine by dropping it in a collection box.

STEP TWO: A postal employee picks up all the letters in the box. He or she delivers them to the local post office.

STEP THREE: Sacks of mail from all over the area are dumped onto a moving belt.

STEP FOUR: A machine prints lines on the stamps so they can't be used again. Each piece of mail gets a postmark. A postmark shows the date and the place where the letter was mailed.

STEP FIVE: Using the zip codes, machines and postal workers sort the mail.

STEP SIX: Letters going to different areas are trucked to the nearest airport. They take a plane ride to get where they're going.

STEP SEVEN: Mail carriers sort the mail for their routes.

STEP EIGHT: Mail carriers deliver the mail on foot or in a car or truck. Your valentine picks up his or her mail—and gets a special message. Happy Valentine's Day!

A word about learning with

Nate the Great

The Nate the Great series is good fun and has been entertaining children for over forty years. These books are also valuable learning tools in and out of the classroom.

Nate's world—his home, his friends, his neighborhood—is one that every young person recognizes. Nate introduces beginning readers and those who have graduated to early chapter books to the detective mystery genre, and they respond to Nate's commitment to solving the case and helping his friends.

What's more, as Nate the Great solves his cases, readers learn with him. Nate unravels mysteries by using evidence collection, cogent reasoning, problem-solving, analytical skills, and logic in a way that teaches readers to develop critical-thinking abilities. The stories help children start discussions about how to approach difficult situations and give them tools to resolve them.

When you read a Nate the Great book with a child, or when a child reads a Nate the Great mystery on his or her own, the child is guaranteed a satisfying ending that will have taught him or her important classroom and life skills. We know that you and your children will enjoy reading and learning from Nate the Great's wonderful stories as much as we do.

Find out more at NatetheGreatBooks.com.

Happy reading and learning with Nate!

Solve all the mysteries with

Nate the Great

- ❑ Nate the Great and the Crunchy Christmas
- ❑ Nate the Great Saves the King of Sweden
- ❑ Nate the Great and Me: The Case of the Fleeing Fang
- ❑ Nate the Great and the Monster Mess
- ❑ Nate the Great, San Francisco Detective
- ❑ Nate the Great and the Big Sniff
- ❑ Nate the Great on the Owl Express
- ❑ Nate the Great Talks Turkey
- ❑ Nate the Great and the Hungry Book Club
- ❑ Nate the Great, Where Are You?

MARJORIE WEINMAN SHARMAT has written more than 130 books for children and young adults, as well as movie and TV novelizations. Her books have been translated into twenty-four languages. The award-winning Nate the Great series, hailed in *Booklist* as "groundbreaking," has resulted in Nate's real-world appearances in many *New York Times* crossword puzzles, sporting a milk mustache in magazines and posters, residing on more than 28 million boxes of Cheerios, and touring the country in musical theater. Marjorie Weinman Sharmat and her husband, Mitchell Sharmat, have also coauthored many books, including titles in both the Nate the Great and the Olivia Sharp series.

MARC SIMONT won the Caldecott Medal for his artwork in *A Tree Is Nice* by Janice May Udry, as well as a Caldecott Honor for his own book, *The Stray Dog*. He illustrated the first twenty books in the Nate the Great series.

HARLEQUIN PINK:
IDOL DREAMS

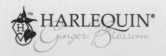

IDOL DREAMS

based on an original novel
by Charlotte Lamb